Volume 2

LAUGH OUT LOUD

Jokes and Riddles from

Highlights for Children

Illustrated by Erin Mauterer

Published by Highlights for Children, Inc.
P.O. Box 18201
Columbus, Ohio 43218-0201
Printed in China

Publisher Cataloging-in-Publication Data (U.S.)

Laugh out loud : jokes and riddles from Highlights for Children /
illustrated by Erin Mauterer.—1st ed.
    p. : ill. ; cm.
ISBN 1-59078-348-4; Vol. 2
1. Riddles, Juvenile. 2. American wit and humor, Juvenile.
I. Highlights for children. II. Title
818.60208 dc22   PN6371.5.L374 2004

First edition, 2004
The text of this book is set in 12-point New Century Schoolbook.

Visit our Web site at www.highlights.com

10 9 8 7 6 5 4 3 2 1

Contents

What kind of dog washes clothes?
A laundromutt.

Mary O'Connor—California

Willie: "My dog hides under the bed when it's bath night."
Gillie: "What's wrong with that?"
Willie: "There isn't room for me."

Brooke Brunson—Georgia

Mr. Johnson walked into a restaurant and was astonished to see a dog paying its bill. "Let me see," said the dog to the cashier. "I owe you $1.20 for the sandwich, 55 cents for milk, and 35 cents for the apple. That comes to exactly $2.00." The dog paid the cashier and left.

Mr. Johnson exclaimed, "I don't believe it! That's the smartest dog I've ever seen."

"Oh, he's not so smart," replied the cashier. "He can't even add correctly."

Rebecca Shumway—Arizona

How does the dogcatcher get paid?
By the pound.

Haylee Porter—Illinois

What is it called when your dog
   sheds hair all over the car?
A haircane.

Jessica Intravia—Connecticut

First dog: "My master calls me
   Tootsie. What does your master
   call you?"
Second dog: "He calls me Sitboy."

Samantha Arnold—Tennessee

Gina: "Don't be afraid of my dog.
   You know the old proverb:
   'A barking dog never bites.'"
Jonathan: "You know it and I
   know it, but does your dog
   know it?"

Steve Grelle—Missouri

What kind of dog says *meow*?
A police dog working undercover.

Graham Boyes—British Columbia

Sue: "I play chess with my dog every day."

Prue: "Wow, your dog must be really smart."

Sue: "Not really. I usually win."

Karina Lassner—Brazil

Did you hear about the neighbor who was so grouchy that her dog put up a sign that said BEWARE OF OWNER?

Katie Koteles—South Carolina

Rick: "Doesn't your dog need a license?"
Lara: "No. I don't let him drive."

José Estrada—California

Sandy: "Try to say 'Richard and Robert purchased a Rottweiler' quickly."
Scott: "Dick and Bob bought a dog."

Susan Qualls—Arizona

Carey: "I'd like to buy that dog, but his legs are too short."

Clerk: "Too short? Why? All four of them touch the ground."

Reed Kufe—Massachusetts

Ben: "This dog must be a good watchdog."

Mary: "How do you know?"

Ben: "He's full of ticks."

Joan Hill—New York

Jeff: "Do you have any dogs going cheap?"

Pet store owner: "No, sir. All of our dogs go *woof*."

Marisa Lemay—Louisiana

What do you call a dog's kiss?
A pooch smooch.

Molly McNutt—Pennsylvania

What kind of dog loves to take
  baths?
A shampoodle.

Ana Kim—California

Sara: "Would you be surprised if you saw your dog chasing a cat?"
Lara: "Yes."
Sara: "Why?"
Lara: "Because I don't have a dog."

Kim Mulder—Alberta

Three reasons why dogs are our most popular pets:
Armadillos are too nosy.
Hippos won't fit through the front door.
You can't walk a goldfish on a leash.

Jon Marx—Wisconsin

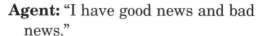

Agent: "I have good news and bad news."

Writer: "First tell me the good news."

Agent: "Paramount loved your story—absolutely ate it up."

Writer: "Great! And the bad news?"

Agent: "Paramount is my dog."

Jessie Davis—British Columbia

What time is it when ten Dalmatians are chasing two poodles?

Ten after two.

Amanda Willard—Massachusetts

What is a dog's favorite movie?
Jurassic Bark.

Rocky Shen—Texas

What is a dog's favorite topping on
    a pizza?
Pupperoni.

Katie Mull—Pennsylvania

What is a dog's favorite prehistoric
   age?
The Bone Age.

Graham Geary—New Hampshire

How do you catch a runaway dog?
*Stand behind a tree and sound like
   a bone.*

Anne Burke—Texas

If every dog has his day, then what
   does a dog with a broken tail
   have?
A weak end.

Tim Feliciano—New Jersey

Why did the man take his dog to
   the railroad station?
To get him trained.

Tanner Swope—Missouri

Why can't Dalmatians play
   hide-and-seek?
They will always be spotted.

Amanda Tenn-Yuk—Florida

Mark: "At the aquarium, I saw a
   dogfish that was part collie."
April: "Why do you think that?"
Mark: "I saw it chase a sea horse
   into the coral."

Shara Ross—New Hampshire

Brenda: "Stop making faces at that bulldog."

Nicole: "Well, he started it."

Nicole Opie—New York

What do you call a dog that works
  for the railroad?
An itch-an-ear.

Amy Green—Missouri

Problem: Your dog chewed up your
  favorite book.
Solution: Take the words right out
  of his mouth.

Jennifer Pacurar—Oregon

Lucy: "Why does your dog turn
  around so many times before he
  lies down?"
Pete: "He's a watchdog, and he's
  winding himself up."

Olga Acebo—Florida

What school did the alphabet go to?
LMN-tary school.

Tyler Busser—South Dakota

All the letters of the alphabet were invited to tea. Which ones were late?

U, V, W, X, Y, and Z, because they came after T.

Irina Lipton Rubenstein—Washington, D.C.

What comes once in a year, never in a month, twice in a week, and never in a day?

The letter E.

Marley Vega—Pennsylvania

David: "What letter comes after *X*?"
Daryl: "*Y*."
David: "Because I asked you."

David Ivery—Georgia

I'm not really there, but still I am seen. There are six letters in my name, and the first one is *M*. What am I?

A mirage.

Emily Reese—California

Which three letters would surprise
the invisible man?
I C U.

Jennifer: "I hope you like the
dictionary I bought you for your
birthday."
Anne: "Yes—I just can't find the
words to thank you."

Jessie Davis—British Columbia

How many letters are in the
alphabet?
*Only twenty-five, because the angel
said, "Noel."*

Tim Rogers—Delaware

Why is a honeysuckle like the
   letter *A?*
Because it's followed by a bee.

Bill Coomes—Kentucky

What letter do you see when you
   look in a mirror?
W (double you).

Nicole Ancona—New Jersey

Why is the letter *T* like an island?
Because it is in the middle of water.

Is there any word with all the
  vowels in it?
Unquestionably.

Rebekah Sykes—Virginia

What comes after *L?*
Bow.

Lauren Wallace—Kentucky

What two letters are always
  jealous?
NV.

Kelsey Bevel—Texas

Railroad crossing—Look out for the cars. Can you spell that without any *R*s?

T-H-A-T.

Katie Shook—North Carolina

What word starts with an *E*, ends with an *E*, and has only one letter in it?

Envelope.

Ankur Garg—Alabama

at five-letter word, when you take away two letters, is left with one?

Stone.

Peter Jancewicz—Quebec

Sarah: "I won 186 goldfish."
Jessica: "Where do you keep them?"
Sarah: "In the bathtub."
Jessica: "What do you do when you want to take a bath?"
Sarah: "I blindfold them."

Shannon Vogel—California

Farmer: "Hey there! What are you doing up in my tree?"

Sam: "Just obeying your sign, sir—the one that says KEEP OFF THE GRASS."

Yasar Sadiq—Michigan

How did the man feel when he
   got a big bill from the electric
   company?
He was shocked.

Meredith Bruyere—Texas

Television repairman: "The
   trouble with your television set
   is a short circuit in the cord."
Woman: "Please lengthen it. I'm
   missing my favorite show."

Meagan Powell—Illinois

Why did the boy keep his bicycle in
   his bedroom?
He got tired of walking in his sleep.

Elisa Richards—Tennessee

Mike: "Red houses are made out of red bricks. Blue houses are made out of blue bricks. What are greenhouses made out of?"

Kelly: "Green bricks?"

Mike: "Greenhouses are made out of glass!"

Zachary Bettschen—Saskatchewan

Father: "We've got twins at our house."

Neighbor: "Really! Are they identical twins?"

Father: "Well, one is but the other isn't."

Rachel Raber—Ohio

Why did the window cry?
Because it had windowpanes.

Ryan Benjamin and
Bill Kamens—Connecticut

Piano tuner: "I'm here to tune your piano."

Marcy: "I didn't call for a piano tuner."

Piano tuner: "I know. Your neighbors did."

Hallie Hamby—Oregon

A brother and sister had a fight and were sent to their rooms. After lying in bed for ten minutes, the brother decided to make up. So he tiptoed down the hall to his sister's room and whispered, "Are you awake?"

"I'm not telling you!" she replied.

Donna Margerum—Pennsylvania

Sister: "Where are you going? Mom said not to walk on the kitchen floor unless your feet are clean."

Brother: "My feet *are* clean. It's my shoes that are dirty."

Tim Larsen—South Dakota

Leah: "Hi, John. Come on in and take a chair."

John: "No, thanks. I already have one at home."

Jim Fairhurst—New Mexico

What gets many answers but never asks any questions?

A doorbell.

Vinnie Zachetti—Pennsylvania

Sareena: "Mom, may I go outside to play?"

Mom: "Have you picked up your room?"

Sareena: "I tried, but it was too heavy."

Adam Sparks—Louisiana

How can you tell if a fly in the
    kitchen is a cowboy?
It'll be on the range.

Demi and Micci Schneider—Illinois

Why did the man put bandages on his refrigerator?
Because it had cold cuts.

Angela Benton—California

Why do ceiling fans go round and
 round?
*If they went up and down, they
 would hit you on the head.*

How is an attic like a vacuum
 cleaner?
They both collect dust.

Chinita Anderson—Washington, D.C.

Jim: "I fell off a hundred-foot ladder
 yesterday."
Matt: "Wow! Aren't you hurt?"
Jim: "No, I fell off the first step."

Matthew Gill—Tennessee

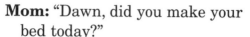

Mom: "Dawn, did you make your bed today?"
Dawn: "Yes, Mom, but I think it would be better to buy one."

Tiffany Renee West—Alabama

Why did Irving disconnect his doorbell?
He wanted to win the No-bell Prize.

Sara Foelker—Wisconsin

Dan: "I was once in a cartoon called 'Breakfast in Bed.'"
Stan: "Did you have a big role?"
Dan: "No—just some toast and jam."

Vincent Williams—Illinois

Why did the boy go to bed with
a hammer?
He wanted to hit the sack.

Mitchell Tutt—Georgia

How can you tell if an elephant has been in your refrigerator?
By the footprints in the butter.

Sarena and Justin Shafner—Connecticut

What is the saddest tool in the kitchen?

The melon baller.

Harrison Cobb—Wisconsin

Donald: "Are you doing the ironing?"

Larry: "No, I'm just having a heated argument with my shirt."

Dawn Riggs—Arizona

James: "Give me a glass of water."

Anna: "Say 'please.'"

James: "Please what?"

Anna: "Please give me a glass of water."

James: "I asked you first."

Mary Reding—Kentucky

When is a door not a door?
When it's ajar.

Christy Tidwell—Tennessee

Mom: "Oh, Mary, please don't put my new rug there."
Mary: "Why not?"
Mom: "Because that's a high-traffic area."
Mary: "Wow, I didn't know cars came into our house!"

Grayland Williams—Ohio

What would you get if you mixed your dad's red paint with black paint?
In trouble.

Sangeetha Nagasivakumaran—Ontario

Cutup Cuisine

Chris: "Why do you carry that tray over your head?"

Waiter: "It's important for everyone to have a balanced meal."

Stephen Rockett—Louisiana

Judge: "Order in the court!"

Russell: "I'll have two cheeseburgers, please."

Jeffrey Williams—South Carolina

First mate: "Who makes the best meals on the ship?"

Second mate: "Captain Cook, of course."

Ned Prutzer—Maryland

Customer: "May I have a hamburger without mustard?"

Waiter: "Sorry, we're all out of mustard. But I can give you a hamburger without ketchup."

Stephanie Newton—Virginia

Customer: "Waiter, this menu is blank on one side."

Waiter: "Well, that's in case you're not very hungry."

Claudia Crespo—New Jersey

Waitress: "Our special today is clams. Would you like to try them?"

Miss Walkfield: "I shell."

Brandi and Catrina Anderson—Florida

What is the best thing to put in a pizza?

Your teeth.

Paul Millett—New York

Waiter: "What would you like for dinner, sir?"

Bob: "A hamburger."

Waiter: "With pleasure!"

Bob: "No, with mustard."

John Frye—Oregon

Susan: "Would you like to join me in a cup of tea?"

Kathleen: "Yes, but I don't think there's room for both of us."

Christian Harrie—California

What do beavers eat for breakfast?
Oakmeal.

Benjamin Lemieux—Quebec

How do you make an egg roll?
You push it.

Eric Lyman—California

Where's the best place on the road
   to stop to eat?
Wherever there's a fork in the road.

Adam Rosemond—North Carolina

What side dish does a miner eat?
Coal slaw.

Kwadjo Asare—Illinois

Little boy: "Hey! You've got a pizza
   on your head!"
Neighbor: "Hmmm. I must have
   eaten my hat for lunch."

Holly Holbrook—Oregon

Student: "I don't like this cheese
with the holes in it."

Cook: "Then just eat the cheese
and leave the holes on your
plate."

Nicholas Pasqua—California

Where does a hamburger go on
Saturday night?

To a meatball.

William Hubbard—Louisiana

Waiter: "Would you like some black
coffee?"

Customer: "No, thanks. Do you
have any other colors?"

Eliezer Abramson—New York

Steak knife: "How do I look?"
Butter knife: "You look sharp, very sharp."

Sara Liebler—Ohio

Mike: "Katie ate four hamburgers in a row!"

Susan: "Wow! She's on a roll!"

Grace Dimond—Maryland

A man walked into a restaurant. "How much for a cup of coffee?" he asked.

"Fifty cents," said the waiter.

"How much for a refill?" asked the man.

"Refills are free," replied the waiter.

"Great!" said the man. "I'll have a refill."

Angela Wood—Virginia

What kind of soda do trees drink?
Root beer.

Jay Nathan—New Jersey

Why does a hummingbird hum?
Because it doesn't know the words.

Raymond Foster—Michigan

What do geologists say about rocks?
"Never take them for granite."

Danny McLeod—Texas

What did one hill say to the other
hill after an earthquake?
"It wasn't my fault."

Brett Cartwright—Missouri

Why is the sky so high?
So birds don't hit their heads.

Carly Richardson—Washington

What kind of bow is impossible to
tie?
A rainbow.

Bobby Renna—Massachusetts

What is a volcano?
A mountain with hiccups.

Scott Brown—British Columbia

What tree grows underwater?
An oaktopus.

Stephanie Mason—New York

How did the mountain climber
feel when he tumbled off the
mountain?
Crestfallen.

Jenny Lin—Hawaii

What do you call an ill tree?
A sickamore (sycamore).

Amanda Tholl—Michigan

Why can't you go more than
halfway into the woods?
Because then you'd be going out.

Colleen Montgomery—New Jersey

Why did the man bury money in his flower garden?
He wanted to make the soil rich.

Michele Tassinari—Massachusetts

What did one mountain say to the
   other mountain?
"Meet me in the valley."

Johnny Pascale—Oregon

Which is braver, a stone or a
   stump?
A stone, because it's a little boulder.

Lindsay Heuertz—Texas

How many oranges grow on an
   orange tree?
All of them.

Bhikhu Patel—Florida

What do you call a scared tree?
Petrified wood.

Sarah Hallforth—Kentucky

Why was the boy surprised when
  he saw celery growing out of his
  ears?
Because he'd planted radishes.

Leigh Manning—North Carolina

How can you identify a dogwood
  tree in the forest?
By its bark.

Ryan Lemke—Wisconsin

What do you call two logs in water?
A pair of swimming trunks.

Michael and Jonathan Lundberg—Louisiana

What is the world's laziest mountain?
Mount Everest.

Alex Meeks—Ohio

What is a frog's favorite flower?
A croakus.

Taylor Lane—Texas

How do birds get ready to exercise?
They do worm-ups.

Connie Shu—Texas

Where is the best place to grow
flowers in school?
In the kindergarten.

LaToya Smith—Georgia

Tourist: "How did these rocks get
here?"
Tour guide: "The glaciers brought
them."
Tourist: "I don't see any glaciers."
Tour guide: "They must have gone
back to get more rocks."

Jennifer Bergermann—Saskatchewan

What plant is cold even in the
summer?
The burr plant.

Whitney Greswold—Massachusetts

What do you call an elderly herb merchant?
An old thymer.

Andrea Kebalo—New York

How did the tree get lost on the highway?
It took the wrong route (root).

Kim Perkins—Massachusetts

What's the smartest mountain?
Mount Rushmore—it has four heads.

Diana Marcelo—Philippines

What kind of tree has hands?
A palm tree.

Alex Valeski—Pennsylvania

Why shouldn't you hug a tree too tight? *It might be the neck of the woods.*

Nicole Pettenati—Ohio

Why are western prairies so flat?
The sun sets on them every night.

Sally Love—Texas

What's tall and smells good?
A giraffodil.

Ruth Schrader—California

What goes snap, crackle, pop?
A firefly with a short circuit.

Erin Landry—Louisiana

What were the trees shouting at
the races?
"We're rooting for you!"

Antonio Tempesta—Massachusetts

Wacky Wheels

What do you call a rabbit that
   works on cars?
A jackrabbit.

Dylan Key—Pennsylvania

What do you call a car that
breathes fire?
A station dragon.

Jasper Chisolm
—Maryland

A man returned to the dealer from whom he bought his new car. "I believe you gave me a guarantee with my car," he said.

"That's right," said the dealer. "We'll replace anything that breaks."

"Good," said the man. "I need a new garage door."

Eilean Guo—California

Bill: "What model is your car?"
Ricky: "It isn't a model. It's a horrible example."

Alexis Jack—New Jersey

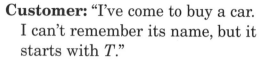

Customer: "I've come to buy a car. I can't remember its name, but it starts with *T*."

Car dealer: "Sorry, we don't have any cars that start with tea. All of ours use gasoline."

Dev Singh—New York

Joe: "Why are you wearing two coats to wax your car?"

Jonathan: "The can said, 'Best performance if you put on two coats.'"

Michael Arnett—Illinois

What is the warmest part of a car? *The muffler.*

Rhianne LeFevre—Connecticut

A man was under the open hood of his car trying to find out why it wouldn't start. His cat was beside him. A neighbor walked by and saw the cat walking around under the hood of the car. He asked, "Is your cat helping you?"

The man replied, "Yes, he is giving the car a cat scan."

Janet Abbene—Virginia

What kind of books do cars read?
Autobiographies.

Christopher Dupont—New York

What would happen if all the cars
   in the country were painted
   pink?
It would be a pink car nation.
Emily Thibodeaux—Rhode Island

Why did the boy stare at the
   automobile's radio?
He wanted to watch a car tune.
David Crockett—California

One day a man's van got very dirty,
so he decided to take it to the car
wash. He got in his van and tried
to start it, but it wouldn't start.

"Oh well," he said, "I'll just take
my car instead."
Michael Peterson—Manitoba

Kelly: "Dad, I can't find my baseball mitt."

Dad: "Maybe it's in the car."

Kelly: "I looked there already."

Dad: "Did you check the glove compartment?"

Patrick Harris—New York

From what kind of dish does a car eat?

A license plate.

Suzanne Huffine—Virginia

Cam: "Did you hear about the man who dreamed he was a muffler?"

Jim: "No. What happened?"

Cam: "He woke up exhausted."

Cam and Jim Dedrick—Ohio

What is a pig's favorite vacation
  spot?
The Pigcific Ocean.

Connor Darcy—Massachusetts

Tanya: "My parents are sending me to camp."

Amanda: "Why? Do you need a vacation?"

Tanya: "No. They do!"

Chris Lugar—California

Andy: "Good news! I've saved up enough money for us to go to Paris this summer."

Sandy: "Wonderful! When are we going to leave?"

Andy: "As soon as I've saved enough for us to come back."

Diane Loya—Texas

Mrs. Brown: "My daughter went on a Caribbean vacation."

Mrs. Gordon: "Jamaica?"

Mrs. Brown: "No, she wanted to go."

Amber Riggins—South Dakota

Ted: "How did you like the cruise?"

Ned: "It was fun, but I didn't approve of the washing machines on the walls."

Ted: "They weren't washing machines; they were portholes!"

Ned: "No wonder I didn't get my clothes back!"

Clare Porter—Michigan

Traveler: "I'd like a room and a bath."

Clerk: "I can give you a room, but you'll have to take your own bath."

Judge Farmer—California

A car filled with tourists drove by two bears at Yellowstone National Park. The bears turned to look at the car.

"What a shame," said one bear to the other. "I think it's awful to keep people caged up like that."

Alan Lara—Texas

Passenger: "Wow! Those people look like ants down there!"

Pilot: "They are ants. We haven't taken off yet."

Crystal Gonzalez—Texas

First woman: "My son came to visit for his vacation."

Second woman: "How nice. Did you meet him at the airport?"

First woman: "Goodness, no. I've known him for years."

Emily Bindl—Wisconsin

If you rowed a boat all day and didn't get anywhere, what did you forget?
To untie the boat.

Melissa Newton—Michigan

What's the best way to start a fire
with two sticks?
*Make sure one of the sticks is a
match.*

David Kramer—New Jersey

When does seven come before six?
In the dictionary.

Christopher Mohnke—Michigan

When you send me, I will not go;
  but when you go, I will follow
  you. What am I?
Your shadow.

Jerry John Owusu—Ghana

I got it in the woods, but couldn't
  find it. The more I looked for it,
  the more I disliked it. I took it
  home because I couldn't find it.
  What is it?
A splinter.

Priscilla Smucker—Pennsylvania

What travels all over the United
  States yet stays in a corner?
A stamp.

Julie Barden—Maine

I'm lighter than a feather yet
   harder to hold. What am I?
Your breath.

It runs all day and never walks;
   often murmurs, never talks; it
   has a bed and never sleeps; has a
   mouth and never eats. What is it?
A river.

Kymberly Strege—Washington

What is green, has four legs, and
   will squash you like a bug if it
   drops out of a tree?
A pool table.

Danny Sedlock—Pennsylvania

Andy: "A man was lost in the desert. Finally, he reached a house, but the only things inside were a bed and a calendar."

Becky: "How did he survive?"

Andy: "He drank the water from the springs in the bed, and he ate the dates off the calendar."

Sarah Keigley—Texas

What cup doesn't hold water?
A hiccup.

Chris Romagna—Massachusetts

Why is a room empty when it is
    filled with married people?
*Because there's not a single person
    in it.*

Christi Powell—North Carolina

What has six legs, four eyes, and
    five ears?
*A man riding a horse and eating
    corn.*

Jennifer Tshudy—Pennsylvania

What is yours but is used mostly by
    other people?
Your name.

Sara Pyle—Kansas

What speaks every language?
An echo.

Diana Holloway—Connecticut

A man left home and made three
   left turns. When he got back
   home, there were two masked
   men waiting for him. Who were
   they?
*The catcher and the umpire. (The
   man was playing baseball.)*

Cody Botzman—Ohio

What house is easy to lift?
A lighthouse.

Lacey and Matthew Chapman
—Maryland

How much dirt is there in a hole
   one foot deep?
None—there's no dirt in a hole!

Jaya Neal—North Carolina

What has six legs and two heads?
A person on a horse.

Michael Birchfield—Virginia

What is small and white and lifts
    weights?
An extra-strength aspirin.

Rueben Romero—California

What kind of shoemaker makes
    shoes without leather?
A blacksmith. He makes horseshoes.

Jessica Goldsborough—Florida

I'm full when I'm gone, and empty
    when I'm here. What am I?
A suitcase.

Shenequa Dore—U.S. Virgin Islands

What do you call a male bug that
  floats?
Buoyant (boy ant).

Timothy Creighton—Pennsylvania

How do slugs begin their fairy
  tales?
"Once upon a slime. . . ."

Jana Smallwood—West Virginia

Why was the father centipede so
  upset?
All his children needed new shoes.

Elizabeth Cavolo—Arizona

Why don't fleas ever catch a cold?
They're always in fur coats.

Casey Bradshaw—North Carolina

What do you call a ladybug's
  husband?
Sir Bug.

Aghavni Dzhugaryan—California

Why did the fly fly?
Because the spider spied her.

Bagha Shams—Gambia

A man heard a knock on his door, but when he opened it, all he saw was a snail. Annoyed, he picked up the snail, carried it really far away, placed it on the ground, and returned home. One year later he heard another knock. When he opened his door, he saw the snail again.

"What did you do that for?" the snail asked.

Jonathan Kuh—California

If a moth breathes oxygen in the daytime, what does it breathe at night?

Nightrogen.

Nikki Herrmann—New Jersey

Why did the spider move from
its home in the window?
It wanted to change Web sites.

Paul Greenwalt—Washington

How does a caterpillar start its
   day?
It turns over a new leaf.

Brandon Barton—South Carolina

Ned: "Don't you ever shoo the mosquitoes?"

Linda: "Nope. I just let them fly barefoot."

Ivan Borrero—New Jersey

What do termites do when they need a rest?

They take a coffee-table break.

Greg Klock—Minnesota

What do you call two spiders that just got married?

Newlywebs.

John Ahn—New York

Why do flies walk on the ceiling?

To take the weight off their legs.

Susan Hamblin—New Brunswick

How do bugs make up their minds?
They pest-decide.

Adam Reifman—California

What is a spider's favorite food at a picnic?
Corn on the cobweb.

David Dobry—Arizona

What happened to the two bedbugs that fell in love?
They got married in the spring.

Jamie Cossette—Connecticut

How do spiders learn definitions?
They study the Web-ster's Dictionary.

Hendrick Pilar—New York

What type of vegetable do bugs
  hate?
Squash.

Hardy Whalen—South Carolina

One day a man went to a pet shop. He asked for a pet that could do everything.

"How about a centipede?" asked the manager.

"I'll take the centipede," said the man.

As soon as the man got home, he asked the centipede to clean the kitchen. In a minute the kitchen was clean.

"Please go to the corner and get a newspaper," the man said.

Five minutes later, no centipede. Forty-five minutes later, still no centipede.

The man went to the front door, and there was the centipede.

"I asked you to go to the corner forty-five minutes ago," said the man.

"I'm going," said the centipede. "I just had to put on my shoes."

Katie Roper—Virginia

What is the worst place for a mosquito?
A room full of clapping people.

Aaron Randall—Texas

How do fireflies begin a race?
"Ready, set, glow!"

Crystal Longo—Massachusetts

What do you call a cricket that says one thing and does another?
A hypocricket.

Cassandra Scott—New York

Why was the knight afraid of the tiny insect?
It was a dragonfly.

Tara Venturini—Pennsylvania

Why did the elephant wear green
  sneakers?
*Because his red ones were in the
  wash.*

Joey Jacks—Illinois

Why can't an elephant ride a
    tricycle?
*Because it doesn't have a thumb to
    ring the bell.*

Christy Ciha—Ohio

Mary: "Peanuts are fattening."
Cary: "How do you know?"
Mary: "Did you ever see a skinny elephant?"

Cristina and Martin Katipunan—Ontario

Why did the elephant sit on the marshmallow?
To keep from falling in the hot chocolate.

Lisa Harrison—Nevada

What has wheels and a trunk but no engine?
An elephant on roller skates.

Sara Mazzoleni—Florida

Fred: "Why do elephants paint their toenails red?"

Lynn: "I don't know. Why?"

Fred: "So when they hide in trees, they'll blend in with the cherries."

Lynn: "But nobody's ever seen an elephant in a tree."

Fred: "See—it works!"

Jacob Neubauer—Minnesota

How do you stop an elephant from going through the eye of a needle?

Tie a knot in its tail.

Sarah Buckleybradley—Vermont

How does an elephant get down
from a tree?
It sits on a leaf and waits until fall.

Michelle Velasquez—New York

How do you know when an
  elephant is under your bed?
*When your nose is touching the
  ceiling.*

Katie Glasser
—Arizona

Why are elephants big, gray, and
  wrinkled?
*If they were small, white, and
  smooth, they would be aspirins.*

Anne Rimkus—Illinois

How do you know an elephant is
  in bed with you?
He's the one with the big E *on his
  pajamas.*

Christian Little—Michigan

How do you find an elephant that's
  hiding in your car?
Check the trunk.

Adam Clarridge—Ontario

How does an elephant climb a tree?
He stands on an acorn and waits
for it to grow.

Ruth Desterke—Florida

Stephanie: "How do you spell
elephant?"
Dan: "*E-l-l-e-e-f-a-n-t.*"
Stephanie: "That's not how the
dictionary spells it."
Dan: "You didn't ask me how the
dictionary spells it."

Trevor Burn—Ontario

What did the elephant do when he
broke his toe?
He called the toe truck.

Molly Kirschbaum—Minnesota

What does a moose get when it lifts
weights?
Big mooscles.

Zach Treacy—Missouri

Why do porcupines love to sew?
They never run out of needles.

Kristie Herlein—Alberta

What do kangaroos have that no
other animals have?
Little kangaroos.

Thomas LaMance—New Mexico

Why was the fox upset?
Because everyone kept hounding him.

Leanna Wilson—Florida

What do you call a camel with no
humps?
Humphrey.

Michael Cook—Texas

Why are swans' necks so long?
*Because their heads are so far from
their bodies.*

Susie Hohman—Maryland

There were two skunks, one named In and one named Out. Once, Out went in and In went out of a store. Then their mother went in and said to Out, "Bring In in."

So Out went out, got In, and they went in. Their mother was happy to see them. She asked Out, "How did you find In so fast?"

And Out said, "Instincts."

Abby Clark—Texas

Where do you find a bear's nose,
    a giraffe's tail, a crocodile's
    stomach, and a zebra's legs?
In the zoo.

Emily Newton—Indiana

Two frogs were sitting on a lily pad, eating lunch. One said to the other, "Time sure is fun when you're having flies."

Derrick Thompson—Maryland

What did the snail say when he went for a ride on the turtle's back?

"Whee!"

Daniel Sumey—Pennsylvania

How do monkeys go down the stairs?
They slide down the banana-ster.

Joey Jacks—Illinois

Why do mother kangaroos hate
  rainy days?
*Because their kids have to play
  inside.*

Amy Reed—Connecticut

Why did the crow sit on the
  telephone wire?
To make a long-distance caw.

Erin Higgins—Florida

How do we know that a
  hippopotamus is sad?
Because of its great size (sighs).

Patricia Scott—Indiana

How do you know that carrots are
   good for your eyes?
*Have you ever seen a rabbit wearing
   glasses?*

Hannah Streeter—Minnesota

A girl opens a box of animal
crackers and takes one out. She
looks at it, then says, "Should we
eat these? The seal is broken."

Lauren Kargoll—Colorado

Why did the dinglehopper cross
   the road?
*It didn't. There's no such thing as a
   dinglehopper.*

Jamila Witmer—Pennsylvania

Why does a stork stand on one leg?
If it lifted both legs, it would fall down.

Stephanie Spigelmoyer—New Jersey

What do you call a hawk that can
　　draw?
Talon-ted.

Breanne Frederick—Colorado

Why does a bear sleep through the
  winter?
Would you wake up a bear?

Aaron Lee—Ohio

What is black and white and lives
  in Hawaii?
A lost penguin.

Julie Reynolds—Maryland

What makes a goose different from
  other animals?
*Most animals grow up, but a goose
  grows down.*

Mark Asher—California

What squawks and jumps out of airplanes?
A parrot-trooper.

Joshua Ricks—Indiana

Which monkey can fly?
A hot-air baboon.

Astley Pitters—Massachusetts

What do you call a kangaroo that's too lazy to leave its mother's pouch?
A pouch potato.

Michael Gwinn—Virginia

What kind of bird wears armor?
A knight owl.

Amanda Mason—Kentucky

What would a gorilla use to fix a
  bike?
A monkey wrench.

Alec Lorraine—Pennsylvania

What happened when five hundred hares got loose on Main Street?
The police had to comb the area.

Tiffany Evans—Virginia

What does a mechanical frog say?
"Ro-bot, ro-bot."

Katelyn Anderson—Minnesota

What do you call a hippo that never stops eating?
Hippobottomless.

Sammie Cox—Pennsylvania

What do you call a turtle that's awake all night?
Nocturtle.

Iza Wojciechowski—Texas

Whiskers and Grins

What is a cat's favorite treat?
Mice cream.

Lindsey Clouse—Indiana

What kind of shoes do mice wear?
Squeakers.

Ibn Shakoor—New Jersey

A woman walked into a store and said, "I need a mousetrap quickly. I have only two minutes to catch a train."

"Sorry," the clerk said. "We don't have any that big."

Rachel West—Illinois

What does a two-hundred-pound mouse say?
"HERE, KITTY, KITTY."

Rachel Cook—Kentucky

What kind of car purrs and has whiskers?
A Catillac.

Ben Hatton—Indiana

Why did the cat put its kittens into
  a drawer?
*It didn't want to leave its litter
  lying around.*

Lindsay York—Indiana

Jennifer: "My cat can talk."
Todd: "No, she can't."
Jennifer: "Yes, she can. I asked
  her what two minus two was, and
  she said nothing."

Lisa Ostrowski—Republic of South Africa

Is it bad luck if a black cat follows
  you?
*It depends on whether you're a man
  or a mouse.*

Josh Brown—Ohio

Where do cats go to look at
   paintings?
The mew-seum.

Kristin Legutki—Connecticut

Hickory, dickory, dock.
Two mice ran up the clock.
The clock struck one,
And the other one got away.

Logan Evans—Alaska

What do you call it when it rains cats?

A great down-purr.

Stephanie Edwards—Oklahoma

Teacher: "Please spell *mouse*."
Meredith: "M-O-U-S."
Teacher: "But what's on the end?"
Meredith: "A tail."

Lorena Arróspide—Belgium

What do cats call their grandfathers?

Grandpaws.

Veronica Taylor—Nova Scotia

Where is a cat when the lights go out?

In the dark.

Gail Klein—New York

Max: "My cat can talk."

Stephanie: "No way! Cats can't talk."

Max: "Mine can. Whenever he gets hurt, he always says, *'Me-ow!'*"

Max Schnitker—Virginia

Customer: "When I bought this cat at your pet shop, you said it was good for mice."

Clerk: "Yes, I did."

Customer: "It doesn't even go near them!"

Clerk: "Well, isn't that good for mice?"

Julie Pajarillo—California

How does a cat keep its mouth
   clean?
With mousewash.

Brent Kosling—Pennsylvania

Father: "What's wrong, son?"

Eddie: "I lost my cat."

Father: "Don't cry. We'll put an ad in the paper."

Eddie: "That won't help. The cat can't read."

Krystal Dulaney—Texas

What kind of cheese would a mouse build his house out of?

Cottage cheese.

Lauren Cooper—Indiana

Bridget: "My cat just had eight kittens."

Erin: "What do you call them?"

Bridget: "Octo-pusses."

Kathleen Panozzo—Michigan

What kind of sauce do sheep use at
  their cookouts?

Baa-baa-cue sauce.

Curt Ganeles—Massachusetts

Audra: "Why are you running a steamroller over your field?"

Jared: "I thought it would be fun to raise mashed potatoes this year."

Lance Beeson—Louisiana

Where do sheep go to get their hair
   cut?
To the baabaa shop.

Joel Perez—Illinois

What do you call a pony that can't
   whinny?
A little hoarse.

Kim Plesek—Iowa

What is another name for a rooster?
A farm alarm.

Meghan Robertson—Pennsylvania

What does a farmer grow when he
   works very hard?
Tired.

Jennifer Clark—Kentucky

What is the worst kind of horse to
   have?
A night mare.

Alex Bruening—Kansas

   A woman was riding a horse
through the woods when she passed
a rabbit.
   "Good morning," said the rabbit.
   The woman rode a little farther,
then said, "I didn't know rabbits
could talk."
   "Neither did I," said her horse.

Jennifer Fleck—Texas

   How did the farmer find his daughter?
He tractor.

Rebekah Bartlett—New York

What do you call a sleeping bull?
A bulldozer.

Jason Luu—Utah

How does a hog write a letter?
With a pigpen.

Michael Gillespie—Florida

What do you call the father of an
   ear of corn?
Popcorn.

Kate Cohen-Barnebey—Washington

Why did the farmer name his pig
   Ink?
It kept running out of its pen.

Robert Groves—Maryland

What did the horse say when she
   finished eating her hay?
"That's the last straw."

Kristina Grbic—New Jersey

What do you put on a bad pig?
Hamcuffs.

Erica Houdek—Illinois

Billy: "Did your pig break her pen?"
Lisa: "Yes. Now she has to type her letters."

Amanda Harris—Louisiana

Baby corn: "Mommy, where did I come from?"
Mother corn: "The stalk brought you."

Delta Gamueda—California

George: "I found a horseshoe."
Jane: "Do you know what that means?"
George: "Yes, some horse is running around in his bare feet."

Natalie Garvey—Georgia

Where do sheep take a bath?
In a baaathtub.

Alexander Taylor—Ontario

What do you call a teeter-totter for a donkey?
A hee-haw seesaw.

Anthony Genco—New York

Boy: "Look at that bunch of cows."
Farmer: "Not bunch—herd."
Boy: "Heard what?"
Farmer: "Of cows."
Boy: "Sure, I've heard of cows."
Farmer: "No, I mean a cow herd."
Boy: "That's OK. I have no secrets from cows!"

Caroline Parrin—Indiana

Farmer: "If you can guess how many chickens I have, I'll give you both of them."

Stacy Wood—Texas

What did one sheep say to the other when it got hurt?
"Are ewe OK?"

Brandon Champion—Mississippi

Billy: "I hear you take milk baths."
Milly: "Yes, I do."
Billy: "Why?"
Milly: "Because I can't find a cow
tall enough to take a shower."

Amanda Lively—Georgia

What is a pig's favorite celebrity?
A hamstar.

Megan Lambert—Utah

How many legs does a horse have if
you call its tail a leg?
*Four. Calling its tail a leg doesn't
make it one!*

Brittany Vetter—Kentucky

What do horses put on their
  burgers?
Mayo-neighs.

Mikhael Klepach—California

Bill: "Tex, why do you wear only one spur?"

Tex: "Well, Bill, I figure if one side of my horse gets going, the other side will come along, too."

Christine Ma—Florida

Knock, knock.
Who's there?
Pasture.
Pasture who?
Pasture bedtime, isn't it?

Matthew Robinson—Kentucky

Clem: "I can't decide whether to buy a bicycle or a cow for my farm."

Lem: "Well, wouldn't you look silly riding a cow?"

Clem: "Yes, but I'd look a lot sillier milking a bicycle."

Krista Neff—Pennsylvania

A man who had lived in the city all his life was visiting a farm. Pointing to a field, he asked the farmer, "Why doesn't that cow have horns? I thought cows had horns."

"Well," said the farmer, "some cows do have horns, and some cows don't. And that cow is a horse."

Veronica Pillar—Virginia

Shauna: "Why did you name your horse Isme?"

Sherri: "So I could say, 'Whoa, Isme!'"

Stephanie Shepherd—Illinois

What do you call a royal horse?
His Majesteed.

Matthew McCanty—Maryland

Teacher: "Stephanie, where is Moscow?"

Stephanie: "In the barn next to Pa's cow."

Clarice Solberg—North Dakota

Cowboy: "Well, sir, did you find the horse to be well mannered?"

Dude: "Yes. Whenever we came to a fence, he stopped and let me go over first."

Becky Brunner—Wisconsin

Rosie: "Did you know that it takes three sheep to make a sweater?"

Posie: "Wow, I didn't even know they could knit."

Daniel Fields—Kansas

Fun by the Numbers

Why do you measure snakes in
  inches?
Because snakes don't have feet.

Monica Zavala—California

What has wings and solves number
  problems?
A mothematician.

Sam Bowler—Illinois

Teacher: "What is a forum?"
Student: "Two-um plus two-um."

Kayla Derfus—Wisconsin

Tony: "Why is a math book always cranky?"
Tina: "I haven't the foggiest."
Tony: "Because it has lots of problems."

Holly Cowderoy—Washington

Mia: "The way I see it, a penny equals one million dollars and a second equals one million years."
Brett: "May I have a penny?"
Mia: "In a second."

Brittany Bode—Louisiana

How many feet are in a yard?
It depends on how many people are standing in it.

Lauren Anderson—Alabama

When one person has six piñon nuts and another person has seven piñon nuts, what do they have?
A difference of a piñon.

Henry Clark—Colorado

What do math teachers do in the lunchroom?
They divide their lunches with one another.

Summer Womack—Kentucky

What did the zero say to the eight?
"Nice belt!"

Stephen Black—Kansas

Which Mexican food is like a ruler?
An inch-ilada.

Mathew Fetterolf—South Carolina

What has a foot on each side and
  one in the middle?
A yardstick.

Jessica Ra—North Carolina

Why is it dangerous to do math in
  the jungle?
*Because if you add four plus four,
  you get ate.*

Angela Kelly—New York

Why is six afraid of seven?
Because seven ate nine.

Matt Chalk—Kansas

What did the 9 say to the 6?
"Why are you standing on your head?"

Asha Anand—Mississippi

Teacher: "If you had thirty-six cents in one pocket and thirty-five cents in the other pocket, what would you have?"

B. J.: "Someone else's pants."

Lora Person—North Carolina

Why was the kitchen having math problems?

Its counter was gone.

Patrick Garth—California

What grew from the plant in the math room?

Square roots.

Carla Wright—Maryland

Say Ahh-ha-ha

What wild animal might you find
in a dentist's office?
A molar bear.

Daniel Tietzer—Illinois

Why did the cookie go to the doctor? *Because it felt crumby.*

Nicholas Zockoll
—Tennessee

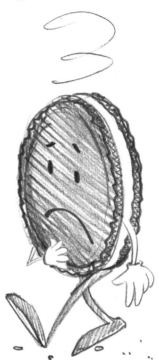

Patient: "Doctor, I keep thinking I'm a frog."

Doctor: "Since when has this occurred to you?"

Patient: "Since I was a tadpole."

Jacob Matsil—Michigan

What two words in a dentist's office can make a toothache go away?

"You're next."

Shawna Holsomback—Georgia

Janet: "Doctor, my brother thinks he's a rubber band."

Doctor: "Well, tell him to snap out of it."

Maria Yannaco—New York

A man walked into a doctor's office with a carrot in one ear and a banana in the other. He said, "I'm not feeling well. Can you help me?"

The doctor said, "Well, I can tell you one thing: You haven't been eating right."

Davey Wreden—California

Woman: "Doctor, I have an awful problem. My husband thinks he's a washing machine."

Doctor: "Well, what's so bad about that?"

Woman: "He doesn't get all the clothes clean."

Diana Lauria—New York

Cowboy: "Doctor, every time I ride a bronco I feel sick. Do you know what it is?"

Doctor: "Bronc-hitis."

David Baker—Arizona

Man: "Doctor, my problem is I think I'm a dog!"

Doctor: "Well, sit down on my couch and we'll talk about this."

Man: "I'm sorry, sir. I'm not allowed on the furniture."

Jonathan Powers—Arizona

Patient: "Doctor, I think I'm a light bulb."

Doctor: "Watt do you mean?"

Elena Pinder—Oregon

Mother: "Doctor, doctor! My son just swallowed a roll of film!"

Doctor: "Let's hope nothing develops."

Nick Khalizadeh—California

Hannah: "Do you have gum in your mouth?"

Rebecca: "No."

Hannah: "Then how do you keep your teeth in?"

Hannah Gribetz—New York

Patient: "I hear an odd noise in my ear—like a phone ringing."
Doctor: "Well, why don't you pick it up?"

Katie Dancey—Pennsylvania

Why do you forget a tooth once it's pulled?
Because it goes right out of your head.

Samantha McKeehan—California

Patient: "I feel funny today. What should I do?"
Doctor: "Become a comedian."

Michael Sesulka—New Jersey

What do you do when your tooth
  falls out?
Get the toothpaste.

David Gaudette—New Hampshire

Mike: "Why are you eating dinner on the corner of the street?"
Patrice: "My doctor said to curb my appetite."

Nichole Hilt—Illinois

What has teeth but never has any
   cavities?
A comb.

Courtney Cecil—Virginia

Patient: "I feel like a deck of cards."
Doctor: "Wait here. I'll deal with
   you later."

Rachel Mitrani—New York

Mother: "Junior, you've lost your
   two front teeth."
Junior: "Oh no, I haven't, Mother.
   I have them in my pocket."

Kelly McKeon—California

Sara fell and broke her arm.
The doctor put it in a sling.

"Will I be able to play the piano
when my arm heals?" Sara asked.

"Sure you will," the doctor
replied.

"That's amazing!" said Sara. "I've
never taken a piano lesson in
my life!"

Hilda Leung—British Columbia

Stacey: "Doctor, you're a genius!
You cured my hearing problem."
Doctor: "Good. That will be sixty
dollars, please."
Stacey: "What did you say?"

Marissa Alexia—California

Why are tooth fairies so smart?
They have a lot of wisdom teeth.

Everett Gifford—New York

Benny: "I keep seeing spots before my eyes."

Barny: "Have you seen a doctor?"

Benny: "No, just spots."

Chris Luong—California

Mother: "Doctor, my son thinks he's a chicken!"

Doctor: "Why didn't you bring him to see me?"

Mother: "I wanted to, but we need the eggs."

Danielle Landry—Maine

What can a dentist's office be compared to?

A filling station.

Nancy Demond—Connecticut

Garden Giggles

What is the singing fruit?
The opera-cot (apricot).

Camille Sciria—Ohio

The Tomato family was walking down the street. Martha, the daughter, walked behind the others, looking at all the people. She didn't see the man on the bicycle, and he accidentally hit her. Mother Tomato came running over and said, "Come on, Martha, ketchup."

Nicole Gilbert—Maine

Who are the police of the fruit
   world?
The apri-cops.

Trevor Wellington—Illinois

What is the saddest fruit?
Blueberries.

Felisha Rogers—West Virginia

Why did the man get fired from the
   orange-juice factory?
Because he couldn't concentrate.

Laura Notarangelo—Massachusetts

Why did the orange stop rolling
   down the hill?
It ran out of juice.

Danielle Jensen—Nebraska

There once were two strawberries in a jar. One strawberry's name was Mary, and the other's was Jack.

Jack said to Mary, "It's all your fault. If you hadn't been so fresh, we wouldn't be in such a jam."

Dana Weinstein—Massachusetts

Why did the cook try to make the cucumber laugh?
To see if it was picklish.

Karina Rodriguez—Arizona

Which vegetables are always going away?
Lettuce leaves.

Joey Huntress—Maine

Why did the banana go out with
the prune?
Because he couldn't get a date.

Lisa Carneal—New Jersey

Why did the orange go to the
  doctor?
She wasn't peeling well.

Holly and Chris Jones—Tennessee

What kind of fruit do scarecrows eat?
Strawberries.

Jennifer and Jaclyn Langer—New Hampshire

What kind of tables do people eat?
Vegetables.

Mark Egger—New York

What do you get if you drop a
basket of fruit?
A mess.

Melissa and T. J. Chism—Pennsylvania

What is orange and keeps falling
off walls?
Humpty Pumpkin.

Tracie Fish—Illinois

What does juice get when it's cold?
Juice bumps.

Christopher Oberholtzer—Virginia

Who writes nursery rhymes and
squeezes oranges?
Mother Juice.

Jennifer Davis—Minnesota

When do you go at red and stop
at green?
When eating watermelon.

Tessa Versteeg—Washington

How do you fix a broken pumpkin?
With a pumpkin patch.

Sarah Cymber—Missouri

What does a banana need to become
  class president?
A peel (Appeal).

Patrick Carney—New York

What happened when the banana
  got into the car?
It peeled out.

How do you make a pumpkin into
  another vegetable?
*Throw it, and it will come down
  squash.*

Devora Einhorn—New York

What did the girl melon say when
  the boy melon asked her to
  marry him?
"We're too young; we cantaloupe."

Ryan Parks—Arizona

Seagoing Sillies

What did the lobster give to its teacher?
A crab apple.

Tonya Neuhuser—Indiana

Where do fish deposit checks?
In a riverbank.

Jennifer Maitland—Florida

What kind of coat does an octopus wear?
A coat of arms.

Joey Ridgeway—Connecticut

What do you do with a blue whale?
Cheer it up.

Shannon Leahy—New York

What does the sea monster eat for dinner?
Fish and ships.

George Hatzisavva—British Columbia

If an athlete gets athlete's foot, what does a scuba diver get?
Under toe (undertow).

Taylor Cooley—Arizona

Why aren't elephants allowed on
the beach?
They can't keep their trunks up.

Sara Capecci—New Jersey

What did the boy get for leaning
over the back of the boat?
A stern warning.

Linda Wilkinson—California

What did the beach say when the
tide came in?
"Long time, no sea."

Rachel Ramos—Texas

Who is an oyster's strongest friend?
A mussel.

Jordan Harrell—North Carolina

What is stranger than seeing a
    catfish?
Seeing a goldfish bowl.

Blayne Kelly—Minnesota

What is the best way to get around
   on the ocean floor?
By taxi crab.

Chelsea Stengel—Indiana

What lives in the ocean and always
   agrees with you?
A seal of approval.

Sergio Marrufo—Texas

What is seaweed's favorite subject?
Algae-bra.

Peter Bruzek—Minnesota

What's the easiest way to catch a
   fish?
Have someone throw it to you.

Ronni Phillips—California

Why do opera singers make good
   sailors?
They know how to handle high C's.

Nicole Jacobsen—Colorado

Two goldfish were in a tank. One goldfish said to the other, "Do you know how to drive this thing?"

Matt Blum—Ohio

Eric: "I just caught a school of fish."
Maria: "Great! What did you use to catch it?"
Eric: "A bookworm."

Donna Phu—California

Megra: "Do you think we should swim here? I heard there were crocodiles."
Peggy: "Don't worry. The sharks scare them away."

Melissa Middleton—Minnesota

What does a
  mermaid sleep on?
A water bed.

Megan Smith—Georgia

Why are fish such poor tennis
   players?
*Because they don't want to get close
   to the net.*

Andrew Rivas—Virginia

What kind of light is used
  underwater?
A floodlight.

Joseph Velez—Florida

Why did the river go on a diet?
It gained a few ponds.

Kacey Czosnowski—Indiana

Who likes to eat at underwater
  restaurants?
Scuba diners.

Jipu Miah—Michigan

What can go through water and
  not get wet?
Sunlight.

Chris Luna—Mississippi

Where does a ship go when it is
  sick?
To the dock.

Mark Goepel—New Jersey

What kind of waves do they have
  on Book Island?
Title waves.

Hannah Haskell—Maine

Why do fish swim in salt water?
Because pepper makes them sneeze.

Javier Mendoza Jr.— Idaho

If you try to cross a lake in a leaky
  boat, what do you get?
About halfway.

April Pfaffe—Minnesota

What did the shark have for lunch?
A roast reef sandwich.

Margaret Shorey—Alaska

What does the tooth fairy bring to
a shark that has lost a tooth?
A sand dollar.

Kyle Bouthilet—Louisiana

What has two knees and lives in
the ocean?
A two-knee fish.

Jeanine Lucia—New York

What do you call a clam that
doesn't share?
A selfish shellfish.

Christin Siemer—California

How do sailors get their clothes
clean?
*They throw them overboard, then
they are washed ashore.*

Cristina and Martin Katipunan—Ontario

Why didn't the fish watch TV?
He was afraid that he'd get hooked.

Katlyn Peugh and Kimberly Almond
—North Carolina

Why does the ocean roar?
*You would, too, if you had lobsters
in your bed.*

Joy Crane—California

How do you divide the sea in half?
With a sea saw.

Yael Bradshaw—New York

How can you communicate with
a fish?
Drop it a line.

Reham Rahman—Minnesota

Alike and Not

Why is a mouse like a clover?
Because the cat'll eat it.

Jay Hashop—Texas

How is a goose like an icicle?
They both grow down.

Denis Malkov—New Jersey

What's the difference between a
   teacher and a train?
*A teacher says, "Spit out your gum,"
and a train says, "Choo, choo,
choo."*

Erin Cadden—Pennsylvania

What's the difference between an
   engineer and a teacher?
*One minds the train and the other
trains the mind.*

Chondra Crosby—South Carolina

What's the difference between a
   smart aleck and a man's question?
*One is a wise guy, and the other is a
guy's why.*

Kirstin Ten Eyck—British Columbia

Why is a pencil like a riddle?
It's no good without a point.

Dayna Hernandez—California

Why is the letter *A* like a flower?
Because a B *always comes after it.*

Alyson Retelback—Alberta

How are a king and a meter stick
  alike?
They are both rulers.

Ryan Shyu—Illinois

What's the difference between ten
  years and a rotten tooth?
*Ten years is a decade and a rotten
  tooth is decayed.*

Crystal Desai—Texas

What's the difference between a
   ballerina and a duck?
*One goes quick on her beautiful
   legs, and the other goes quack on
   her beautiful eggs.*

Jocelyn Rae Helmig—British Columbia

What's the difference between a
  coat and a baby?
*A coat is what you wear; a baby is
  what you were.*

Shruti Gokhale—India

What's the difference between
a coyote and a flea?
One howls on the prairie; the other
prowls on the hairy.

Anna Borkowski—Massachusetts

Jessica: "What's the difference
between a paper shredder and
a mailbox?"
Allen: "I don't know."
Jessica: "Well, I'll never send you
out to mail a letter!"

Lindsay Robinson—Missouri

Why is an airline pilot like a
running back?
Both want to make a touchdown.

Katie Blount—Texas

What is the difference between a
   water-balloon toss and an egg
   toss?
*In a water-balloon toss you get
   soaked, in an egg toss you get
   yolked.*

Jessica Budinger—Ohio

What is the difference between
   a person with a cold and a
   prizefighter?
*One blows his nose, the other knows
   his blows.*

Joe Shrift—Pennsylvania

How is a cake like a baseball team?
Both need a good batter.

Chayie Werczberger—New York

Tick-Tock Ticklers

What did the big hand on the clock
   say to the little hand?
"I'll be back in an hour."

Nathan Davis—North Carolina

When did the knife get home?
At eight o'clock sharp.

Lansing Salvas—Massachusetts

Sue: "Does your watch tell time?"
John: "No. You have to look at it."

Erica Oh—New York

Jack: "What time is it?"
Tim: "I don't know."
Jack: "Well, what does your watch say?"
Tim: "Tick-tock, tick-tock."

Argie Velez—Washington

Jenny: "Hey, Whitney, you know that watch you gave me for my birthday?"
Whitney: "Yes."
Jenny: "I had to put it in the shop because it had ticks."

Jenny Tyler—Texas

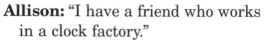

Allison: "I have a friend who works in a clock factory."

Andy: "What does he do?"

Allison: "He stands around all day and makes faces."

Mirakel Mayoral—Massachusetts

Doctor: "Good heavens! There's a wristwatch in your stomach!"

Dave: "Yes, I know. I swallowed it when I was twelve."

Doctor: "Does it give you any trouble?"

Dave: "Only when I wind it."

Owen Gregory—Missouri

Why did the teacher send the clock
  to the principal's office?
For tocking too much.

Nafees Ahmed—Oklahoma

Three friends climb to the top of Big Ben to throw their watches off the top, then run to the ground to catch them. The first man throws his watch and takes five steps before his watch hits the ground and breaks. The second man throws his watch and takes only three steps before his watch lands and breaks.

Finally, the third man throws his watch, then walks down the stairs and buys a snack before catching his watch. His friends ask him how he did it, and he says, "My watch is thirty minutes slow."

Taylor Hodge—Virginia

Say That Again?

What did the baby porcupine say to
   the cactus?
"Is that you, Mama?"

Derek Dueñez—California

What did the sardine say when he saw the submarine?

"Look! There's a can of people."

Angela DeVries—Florida

What did one pencil say to the
other pencil?
*"You're sharp, but please get to the
point."*

Michael Henderson—Texas

What did the mother pill say to the
baby pill when the guests
arrived?
"Aren't you going to vitamin?"

Emily Humphreys—Virginia

What did one snake say to the
other?
*"Let's see you worm your way out
of this one."*

Kyle Fedderson—South Dakota

What did one camera say to the
other when it saw something
interesting?
"That's flash-inating."

Bethany Clements—Texas

What does a chickadee say when
it's very hungry?
"Long time, no seed."

Kimberly Kastner—New York

What did the broom say to the
vacuum cleaner?
*"I wish people would stop pushing
us around."*

Timothy Zumwalt—Oregon

What did the bowl say to the
    spoon?
"What are you stirring at?"

Andrew Krol—Ontario

What did one worm say to the
other worm?
"Where on earth have you been?"

Debbie Kunjachan—New York

What did the tie say to the hat?
"You go on ahead, I'll just hang around."

Arif Islam—Texas

What did summer say to spring?
"Help! I'm going to fall!"

Angie Clintsman—Wisconsin

What did the painter say to the wall?
"One more crack like that and I'll plaster you."

Eric Ford—Kentucky

What did one shoe say to the other?
"Don't people just wear you out?"

Nancy Lynch—South Carolina

What did the heater say to the
    freezer?
"Have an ice day."

Becca Albers—Illinois

What did the glove say to the
    baseball?
"Catch you later!"

Courtney Sellars—Tennessee

What did the bed say to the wind?
"Are you trying to blow my cover?"

Lance Merlo—Texas

What did the plant say to the
    gardener?
"Take me to your weeder."

Sean Conroy—North Carolina

What did one magnet say to the
  other magnet?
"I find you very attractive."

Hannah Robinson—Alabama

What did the fish say to its friend
   after the drought?
"Long time no sea!"

Julie Lazar—California

What did the happy light bulb say
to the sad light bulb?
*"Why don't you lighten up, my
friend?"*

Tera Lea Gwaltney—Tennessee

What did the gerbil say when he
went to the bank?
*"Be careful—this is my life
shavings."*

Stephanie Held—Texas

What did one flea say to the other?
*"Shall we walk or take the greyhound
to town?"*

Chuckie Thomas—Michigan

What would you say to a
  boomerang on its birthday?
"Many happy returns!"

Whitney Sickels—Florida

What did the mother ghost say to
  her children when they got into
  the car?
"Put on your sheetbelts."

Krystal Anstey—Newfoundland

What did the piano say to the
  angry metronome?
"Tempo, tempo, tempo!"

Gary Fayman—New Jersey

What did the robot say to the gas
  pump?
*"Take your finger out of your ear
  and listen to me!"*

Alyssa Padgett—Kentucky

What did one washing machine say to the other?

"Let's go for a spin."

Ryan Batts—North Carolina

What did one elevator say to the other?
"I think I'm coming down with something."

Oriana Farnham—Ohio

What did the bee say to the flower?
"Hi, bud!"

Craig Baker—Tennessee

What did one leaf say to the other?
"Have a nice fall."

Kishan Thadikonda—Maryland

What did the tree say when it couldn't solve the riddle?
"I'm stumped!"

Sarah Ann Stoltzfus—Pennsylvania

What did the calculator say to the student?

"You can count on me."

Brandon Tate—Louisiana

What did the sea say to the ocean?

Nothing, it just waved.

Leigh Kaminski—Florida

What did the father buffalo say to his son when he was leaving?

"Bison."

Carla Snodgrass—Tennessee

What did the picture say to the wall?

"I've been framed!"

Amanda Evans—Texas

What did the tree say when spring
   came?
"What a re-leaf!"

Jennie Rocheleau—Wisconsin

What did the big firecracker say to
   the little firecracker?
"My pop is bigger than yours."

Kevin Bolton—Tennessee

What did one rocket say to the
   other rocket?
"Let's go to launch."

Philip Hurley—Florida

What did one plate say to the
   other?
"Lunch is on me."

Lisa McGee—California

What did Cinderella say when she
was waiting for her photos?
"Someday my prints will come."

Patrick Fox—North Carolina

What is a clown's favorite snack?
Peanut riddle.

Madeleine Clark—North Carolina

Why was the kid at the party cold?
Because it was a brrrr-thday party.

Ari Brill—New Jersey

Little boy (to store clerk): "Have you seen a woman without a little boy who looks like me?"

Melissa Toews—Manitoba

Dad: "Adam, what do you want for your birthday?"
Adam: "I can't tell you, or it wouldn't be a surprise."

Paul Cohen—Missouri

Why is a police officer so strong?
Because he can hold up traffic.

Lauren Clarkson—California

Jim: "What's white, steep, and has ears?"

Tara: "I don't know."

Jim: "A snow-covered mountain."

Tara: "What about the ears?"

Jim: "Haven't you ever heard of mountaineers?"

Jimmy Hughes—Massachusetts

What do chess players have for breakfast?
Pawncakes.

Michael Ross—Maryland

What did Paul Revere say at the end of his ride?
"Whoa!"

Marilyn Buck—Indiana

What's the most artistic part of a
  castle?
The drawbridge.

Chlump Chatkupt—New Jersey

Why did the germ cross the
   microscope?
To get to the other slide.

Ryan Duncan—Ohio

What does Teacher Rabbit read to
  her bunnies?
Hare-raising stories.

Nathan Bradshaw—Massachusetts

What did the hot dog say when it
   finished the race first?
"I'm the wiener!"

Billy Chapman—Florida

How did the Vikings send messages?
Norse code.

Mathew Adkins—Massachusetts

Secretary: "The Invisible Man is here to meet with you."
Boss: "Tell him I can't possibly see him!"

Ernestine Talibsao—Saudi Arabia

Two atoms were walking down the street. One said, "I lost an electron!"

"Are you sure?" asked the other.

"I'm positive," said the first.

Jarred Breidenstein—Pennsylvania

A woman sent her dog to college. The dog failed math but got an A in foreign languages. The woman said, "If you're so good in foreign languages, let me hear you say something in a foreign language."

The dog said, *"Meow."*

Erin Vosbrink—Missouri

What do you call a person who is always wiring for money?
An electrician.

John Coppola—New Jersey

What color is rain?
Water-color.

Joyce Sank—Pennsylvania

Two ants were running across the top of a cracker box. One stopped and said, "Hey, why do we have to run so fast?"

"Can't you read?" said the other ant. "It says TEAR ACROSS THE DOTTED LINE."

Karra Hurkett—Michigan

What is as big as an elephant but
    weighs nothing?
An elephant's shadow.

Roger Gelwicks—Indiana

Mom: "Why didn't you take the bus home?"

Andy: "I tried, but it wouldn't fit in my backpack."

Faye Castillo—Hawaii

How would you know if you had a toadstool in your trash can?
There wouldn't be mushroom inside.

Jacob Goldschlager—Australia

Sabrina: "Are there eggs on the menu?"

Waiter: "No. We clean the menus every day."

Amanda Day—Missouri

Why didn't the man play cards
   during his ocean cruise?
*Because the captain was standing
   on the deck.*

   Kelly and Jason Criss—South Carolina

Boss: "I see you had a good
   vacation."
Worker: "Not too bad, but it rained
   the whole time."
Boss: "At least you got a tan."
Worker: "It's not a tan. It's rust."

   Susan Simonson—Saskatchewan

Gina: "I've been swimming since I
   was five years old."
Randy: "You must be tired!"

   Amanda Butler—Ohio

What do cats say when they want
to go outside?
"Me out."

Dave Mihulka—Colorado

Where are french fries born?
Greece (grease).

Ryan Walsh—Ohio

Who is a pizza's favorite relative?
Aunt Chovy (anchovy).

Michelle Williams—Michigan

Mother: "Do you want any more
ABC soup, honey?"
Daughter: "No, thanks. I couldn't
eat another syllable."

Ryan Kiecker—Minnesota

What was the tow truck doing at
the racetrack?
Trying to pull a fast one.

Jennifer Keefe—Florida

What is a zookey?
A key to the zoo.

Beverly Klimkowsky—New York

Share the Fun

Want us to consider your favorite joke or riddle for publication in *Highlights for Children* magazine?

Send us the funniest joke or the best riddle you've ever heard, with your name, age, and full address (number and street, city or town, state or province, and Zip Code), to:

> *Laugh Out Loud*
> Highlights for Children
> 803 Church Street
> Honesdale, Pennsylvania 18431